5|8|17

To Elena

Just a little gift
for you.

Kath x

© 2017 Rain Wilson
All rights reserved

This book is a work of fiction and the names, characters
(with the exception of Julian, who is a real dog) and
events are either the product of the author's imagination
or are used fictitiously. Any resemblance to actual
persons, living or dead or events is entirely coincidental.

Photography by Halina Fuller
Illustrations by Katherine Parker

ISBN - 13: 978-1546728368
ISBN – 10: 1546728368

Julian's Dream

Written by Rain Wilson
&
Illustrated by Katherine Parker

Ireland 2017

This book is dedicated to animal rescue workers everywhere.

Every Dog
Has a Dream

The Story of a Rescued Dog and His Dream

Julian the dog lives in Sunny Lawns, the home for rescued dogs and cats. He hurt his foot before he came to live here but it is nearly better now, although he still has to wear a bandage.

The people are all very kind in Sunny Lawns but Julian wishes he could go and live in a house. He has heard from the other dogs that many of them leave here to live in houses which are called Forever Homes. The dogs have told him you have to be chosen.

Julian lives in a kennel with a bowl of water, a bed to sleep in and a soft blanket. He can see a road from his kennel with cars going up and down all day. The best part of Julian's day is when he sees a tractor going by with a farm dog sitting on the back. It is Julian's dream to ride on a tractor like a farm dog.

One night Julian can't sleep. He is worried in case his dream never comes true. The sound of wings flapping makes him look up. A beautiful white owl lands on the ground next to his kennel. 'Keep believing in your dream, Julian' says the owl. Then the owl flies away into the dark sky.

One day a nice lady comes to Julian's kennel, scratches his ears and calls him a good dog. She talks to the lady from Sunny Lawns about Julian. The dog in the next kennel tells him he has been chosen. Julian is very excited. Then he is taken to the lady's car. Julian is so happy he falls asleep on the comfortable back seat.

When he wakes up, Julian is in his new home. He has a new bed by the fire and a new water bowl and best of all, a new collar and a lead. In his new home he meets the cat who is called Neil. Neil likes to play but runs away if Julian chases him. Julian loves Neil and his new home.

Every morning a red tractor drives past the house with a farm dog on the back. It comes back along the road again a bit later. Julian sits at the gate watching, very excited. It is still his dream to ride on a tractor. Neil says that sometimes the tractor stops and that Julian could ask the farm dog if he will swap places with him.

Julian's foot is better now and he doesn't have to wear the bandage. He watches every morning for the farm dog to go past on the tractor. One day the tractor stops. The farmer is talking to another man on the road. Julian slips out of the gate and jumps up onto the tractor beside the farm dog. The farm dog says his name is Finbar.

Finbar says he would like to lie in front of a warm fire for the day so the two dogs swap places. Finbar goes into Julian's house and Julian sits up on the back of the tractor. The farmer does not notice he now has a different dog on the back. Julian is very happy and proud as they drive to the farm. This is the best day of his life.

When Julian gets to the farm he jumps down from the tractor. The farmer is busy and still doesn't notice that Julian is not Finbar. Julian sees some big animals. They are cows. The cows moo loudly and walk over to sniff Julian with their hot breath. He is frightened and runs away.

Next, Julian gets chased by some chickens. They have lots of feathers and sharp yellow beaks. They peck at him and make loud squawking noises. They have laid eggs and don't want them to get broken by a big clumsy dog.

The sun is shining and it is a lovely warm day. Julian sees a field full of yellow haystacks. He chooses the biggest haystack. He climbs to the top and then slides down the other side. It is soft when he lands. It is so much fun he does it over and over again.

24

Then he sees some round pink animals. They are pigs. The pigs are happy and smiling and roll on their backs in the mud. Julian rolls in the mud too. Some woolly sheep are in the next field. They see Julian rolling around and all run into the corner of their field saying, 'Baa, baa!'

Julian runs on and comes to the stable yard where a big cart horse is eating some hay. The horse is much taller than Julian and has a long mane and tail. The horse wants to be friends. Julian tastes the hay but it is dry and stringy and not nice to eat.

Then he notices the farmer getting back onto the tractor. So Julian jumps aboard and is soon chugging down the lane back to his house. His ears blow back in the wind and he feels very important. Riding on the back of the tractor is his favourite part of the day. Julian has never been so happy.

When they come to Julian's house, he jumps down. Finbar comes out of the gate and jumps up in his place. 'Thank you for changing places with me! I had a lovely time,' shouts Julian as the tractor drives away. Finbar waves happily. He has had a nice day too, snoozing in Julian's bed.

Julian is quite tired now and gets straight into his bed but his owner shouts, 'Julian! Where did you get so muddy? You MUST have a bath.' He is washed in a warm bath. The bubbles are soft and smell nice. When he is lifted out of the bath he is lovely and clean. At last he lies down in his bed in front of the fire.

Julian is so tired after his adventure that he falls straight to sleep. He dreams happy dreams for the rest of the night, all about the day his dream came true. It was wonderful to be a farm dog riding on a tractor. As he dreams, his paws twitch ever so slightly and his tail thumps gently on the blanket.
The owl was right!

Contact:
rainwilson@eircom.net
parkercartoonart@outlook.com

Website:
https://halinafuller.wixsite.com/juliansdream

I am Julian the lurcher and this is my story.

21852479R00027

Printed in Great Britain
by Amazon